MY DADDY AND ME

For Dad—
'Cause we go together
—A.E.S.

To my grandfathers,
Lloyd Milton Hansen
and Israel Ard Hoyt
—A.H.

ISBN 0-439-74046-0

Text copyright © 2005 by Amy E. Sklansky.

Illustrations copyright © 2005 by Ard Hoyt.

All rights reserved. Published by Scholastic Inc.

SCHOLASTIC, CARTWHEEL BOOKS, and associated logos

are trademarks and/or registered trademarks of Scholastic Inc.

10 9 8 7 6 5 4 3   06 07 08 09

Printed in the U.S.A. 23 • First printing, June 2005

The illustrations for this book were done in watercolor, colored pencil, and pen and ink on Arches paper.
The text was set in Hank BT, and the display type is Smile ICG Medium.

MY DADDY AND ME

Written by Amy E. Sklansky • Illustrated by Ard Hoyt

SCHOLASTIC INC.

New York   Toronto   London   Auckland   Sydney
Mexico City   New Delhi   Hong Kong   Buenos Aires

We go together
like honey and bees,
like peanut butter and jelly,

like hide-and-seek.

Whatever the weather,
we go together.

We go together
like wind and kites,

like pail and shovel,

like moon and stars.

Whatever the weather,
we go together.

We go together
like rakes and leaves,

like boots and rain,

like hugs and kisses.

Whatever the weather,
we go together.

We go together
like coats and hats,

like skates and ice,
like cocoa and marshmallows.

Now and forever—

My daddy and me,
we go together!